Note to parents, carers and teachers

Read it yourself is a series of modern stories, favourite characters and traditional tales written in a simple way for children who are learning to read. The books can be read independently or as part of a guided reading session.

Each book is carefully structured to include many high-frequency words vital for first reading. The sentences on each page are supported closely by pictures to help with understanding, and to offer lively details to talk about.

The books are graded into four levels that progressively introduce wider vocabulary and longer stories as a reader's ability and confidence grows.

Ideas for use

- Although your child will now be progressing towards silent, independent reading, let her know that your help and encouragement is always available.

- Developing readers can be concentrating so hard on the words that they sometimes don't fully grasp the meaning of what they're reading. Answering the puzzle questions at the back of the book will help with understanding.

For more information and advice on Read it yourself and book banding, visit www.ladybird.com/readityourself

Book Band
10

Level 4 is ideal for children who are ready to read longer stories with a wider vocabulary and are eager to start reading independently.

Special features:

Detailed illustrations to capture the imagination

Clear type

Longer sentences

Full, exciting story

Richer, more varied vocabulary

The sun came up over Piggy Island. It was a new day – the day of the Great Fling-Off. The excited birds made their way to the slingshot in time for the start of the competition.

But where were Red and Chuck?

"It's no good!" said Red. "We must get the eggs back!"

The other birds were all at the Fling-Off. Only Chuck and Red could save the nest.

"Let's get old helmet-head first!" said Chuck. They set off after Corporal Pig.

Educational Consultant: Geraldine Taylor
Book Banding Consultant: Kate Ruttle

A catalogue record for this book is available from the British Library

This edition published by Ladybird Books Ltd 2014
80 Strand, London, WC2R 0RL
A Penguin Company

001

The moral right of the author and illustrator has been asserted.

ISBN: 978-0-72328-905-0

Printed in China

Red and the Great Fling-Off

Written by Richard Dungworth
Illustrated by Ilias Arahovitis

Red couldn't sleep. He was too excited. The next day was the day of the Great Fling-Off on Piggy Island. Last year, Chuck had been the winner. "But this year," thought Red, "it's my turn!"

The Fling-Off was the birds' big
competition. They took turns to
fling themselves as far as they could
with the slingshot. The one who
went furthest was the winner.
Red had practised his fling over
and over again.

"But what if Chuck has practised more?" thought Red.
Chuck loved competitions. He loved all the training and practising.
He loved to come first, too.

"Perhaps I should do some more training right now," thought Red.

Red made his way quietly to the slingshot. But Chuck had got there first. Just like Red, Chuck was too excited to sleep. Just like Red, he had got up in the night to do some more training.

"Great!" said Chuck. "Now we can train together!"

Red didn't want to help Chuck train. He wanted to be the Fling-Off winner this year. But he couldn't see a way out.

"Let's start with speed training!" said Chuck. "I'll race you to the top of the mountain. Go!"

The race was very close. Chuck just made it to the mountain top first. Red was going so fast, he went TOO far!

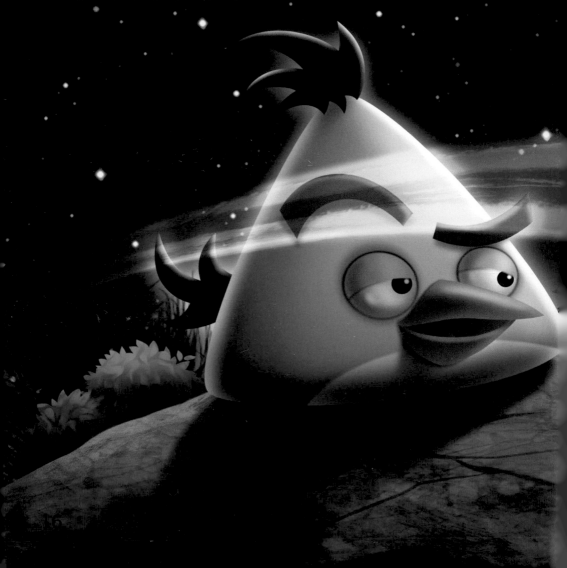

By now, Red was a very angry bird!
"Right!" he said to Chuck. "Let's
see how well you can swim! See that
big rock out there? The first one to
swim there and back is the winner!"

The race was close again. But this time, Red came first. Chuck didn't like that.
"We should test our strength next," he said. So the two birds had another competition.

And then another...

and then another...

The sun came up over Piggy Island. It was a new day – the day of the Great Fling-Off. The excited birds made their way to the slingshot in time for the start of the competition.

But where were Red and Chuck?

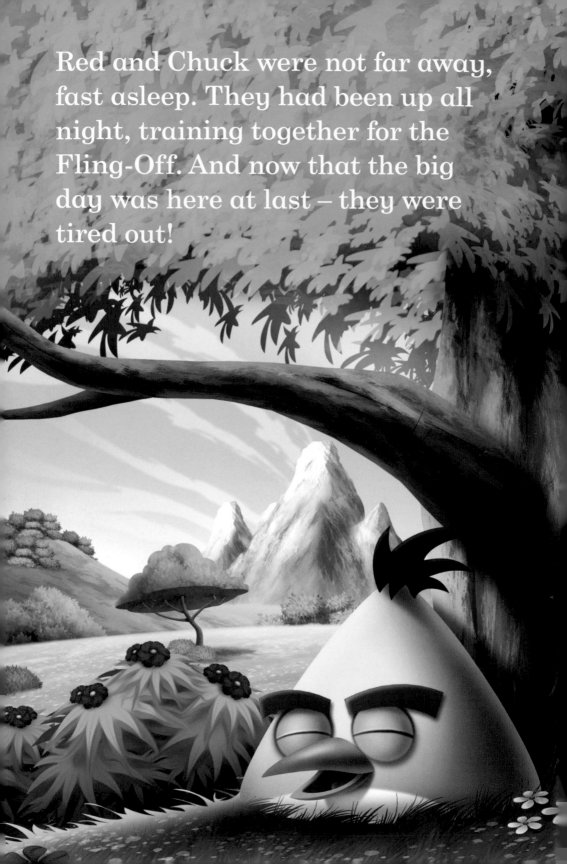

Red and Chuck were not far away, fast asleep. They had been up all night, training together for the Fling-Off. And now that the big day was here at last – they were tired out!

Chuck woke up. "Get up, Red!" he said. "The Fling-Off must be about to start!"

They set off for the slingshot at top speed. But on the way, Red saw something. "Look!" he said quietly. "Over there! Pigs!"

Corporal Pig and three other pigs were sneaking away from the birds' home. They had something with them – something that made Red and Chuck very angry.

"They are sneaking away with our nest!" said Red.
"And the eggs!" said Chuck.

Red and Chuck were about to go after the pigs when they heard a noise. It was the noise that marked the start of the Fling-Off. Chuck and Red looked at one another. They were about to miss the competition.

"It's no good!" said Red. "We must get the eggs back!"

The other birds were all at the Fling-Off. Only Chuck and Red could save the nest.

"Let's get old helmet-head first!" said Chuck. They set off after Corporal Pig.

Corporal Pig made it as far as the mountain. He raced up it as fast as he could. But Chuck and Red were much faster. They soon had the nest back.

"Now for the eggs!" said Red.

The first minion pig thought he would float away. But Red thought not. He could swim much faster than a pig could float! He soon had the first egg back.

"Only two more to go!" he said to Chuck, as he put it in the nest.

37

Chuck didn't use speed to catch the next minion pig. He used his strength – and a very big rock. Soon there were two eggs back in the nest.

"Just one more to save!" said Red with a smile.

Red and Chuck were tired from training all night. But they were not about to let the last pig get away with their egg. Together, they used the last of their speed and strength to catch him.

Red and Chuck were both very glad the nest was full again – but sad they had missed the Fling-Off.

"Perhaps one of us will be the winner next year," said Chuck.
"Yes," said Red. "But which one?"

"Don't start that again!" said Matilda. The other birds had come racing over to see Red and Chuck. They were all smiling.

"We saw how you saved the eggs just now," said Matilda. "And that makes you both winners!"

How much do you remember about the story of Angry Birds: Red and the Great Fling-Off? Answer these questions and find out!

- What competition does Red want to win?

- Who does Red want to beat?

- Who wins the race to the mountain top?

- Who wins the swim to the rock and back?

- How many eggs do the pigs steal?

- Who tells Red and Chuck they are both winners?

Unjumble these words to make characters from the story, then match them to the correct pictures.

Rde   Croprlao Pgi

Miladat   Cukhc

Read it yourself with Ladybird

Tick the books you've read!

For more confident readers who can read simple stories with help.

Level 3

- YOU won't like this present as much as I DO!
- The Elves and the Shoemaker
- Hansel and Gretel
- Harry and the Bucketful of Dinosaurs
- Jack and the Beanstalk
- The Red Knight
- Furi on Music Island
- Poppet Stows Away
- Rapunzel
- Aladdin
- The Jungle Book
- Roxy and the Great Escape
- ANGRY BIRDS CHEER UP, CHUCK!
- ANGRY BIRDS BOMB'S BEST BIRTHDAY

Longer stories for more independent, fluent readers.

Level 4

- I am Inventing an INVENTION
- Harry and the Dinosaurs United
- Heidi
- Katsuma and the Art Thief
- Luvli and the Glump-a-tron
- The Pied Piper of Hamelin
- Sam and the Robots
- Snow White and the Seven Dwarfs
- The Wizard of Oz
- The Little Mermaid
- Alice in Wonderland
- Oddie The Hero
- ANGRY BIRDS RED AND THE GREAT FLING-OFF
- ANGRY BIRDS STELLA